THE VERY CRANKY BEAR

NICK BLAND

Hodder
Children's
Books

A division of Hachette Children's Books

In the Jingle Jangle Jungle on a cold and rainy day,
four little friends found a perfect place to play.

Moose had marvellous antlers and Lion, a golden mane.
Zebra had fantastic stripes and Sheep . . . well, Sheep was plain:

THE VERY CRANKY BEAR

015

To Tom and Sam. NB.

First published in 2008
by Scholastic Australia

This edition first published in the UK in 2009
by Hodder Children's Books

Text and illustrations copyright © Nicholas Bland 2008

Hodder Children's Books
338 Euston Road
London NW1 3BH

A catalogue record of this book is available from the British Library.

HB ISBN: 978 0 340 98942 5
PB ISBN: 978 0 340 98943 2

10 9 8 7 6 5 4 3 2 1

Printed in Singapore

Hodder Children's Books is a division of Hachette Children's Books
An Hachette UK Company
www.hachette.co.uk

None of them had noticed that someone else was there.

Sleeping in that cave was a very cranky . . .

BEAR!

'ROAAAAR.' went the cranky bear,
'ROAR. ROAR. ROAR!'

He gnashed his teeth and stomped his feet
and chased them out the door.

So in the Jingle Jangle Jungle on a cold and rainy day,
four little friends had nowhere warm to play.

'Wait a minute,' said Zebra,
as she scratched her furry chin.
'Maybe if we cheered him up,
he'd let us come back in.'

'If I did not have stripes,' said Zebra,
'I'd be cranky too.
We should give that bear some stripes,
that's what we should do.'

'Stripes are silly,' Moose complained,
'especially on a bear.
My antlers always cheer me up,
let's give that bear a pair.'

'No, no, no, no, no,' said Lion,
'antlers are a bore!
A golden mane like mine,' he said,
'would cheer him up for sure.'

So Zebra fetched a tin of mud
and Lion, some grass of gold.

Moose got two big branches,
and Sheep . . . well, Sheep got cold.

Sheep was getting worried.
'They've been eaten up for sure!'

And then, from in the cave,
there came a very cranky . . .

'ROAAAAR'.

Zebra, Lion and Moose ran out and Bear was right behind them.
They hid behind the bushes where they hoped he wouldn't find them.

'Why is he still cranky, he's got antlers, stripes and mane?
Before we gave him those,' Lion said, 'he looked so very plain!'

As Bear stormed back inside the cave,
he turned and roared at Sheep.

'ALL I REALLY WANT,' he said,

'IS A QUIET PLACE TO SLEEP!'

So she fetched a pair of clippers
and she clipped off half her wool.

She stuffed it in a cotton bag
until the bag was full.

She tiptoed back inside the cave. 'Excuse me, Bear,' she said.
'Would you like a pillow for underneath your head?'

'Well, thank you very much,' said Bear and soon he fell asleep.
Maybe he was dreaming of a plain, but thoughtful sheep.